THE FAIRIES OF
THE HOLLOW HILLS

By Jan Kuśmirek

Published by New Generation Publishing in 2019

Copyright © Jan Kuśmirek 2019

First Edition

The author asserts the moral right under the Copyright, Designs and Patents Act 1988 to be identified as the author of this work.

All Rights reserved. No part of this publication may be reproduced, stored in a retrieval system or transmitted, in any form or by any means without the prior consent of the author, nor be otherwise circulated in any form of binding or cover other than that in which it is published and without a similar condition being imposed on the subsequent purchaser.

ISBN: 978-1-78955-459-5

www.newgeneration-publishing.com

For Shirley and Tilde

With thanks to Nicola Clare Lydon & Lynne Tansey
2018

CHAPTER 1

Reality

Fairyland is a strange place indeed. It comes and it goes, and people say it floats beyond reach, or it hides in mists, or suddenly appears but in fact it is just around us, quite normal and ordinary, if you are a fairy or of fairy blood.

Fairy blood? How can that be? Sometimes by hook and by crook, for a year and a day, a fairy consorts with mortal beings and a golden child comes, blessed with the sight, or even charm and wit beyond most mortals. And there is the difference, clear to see in the name mortal, for fairies are the folk of time where time means little; a thousand years may just seem a year.

As with mortal beings the Fay come in many forms and in many tribes and we give them many names and characters. But those who consort and join with us, these are the Lordly Ones, the people of the hollow hills the raths and high places. They are those who have affection for humankind, they who desire a mortals touch; and so the Fay enchant mortals and inspire them. It was the Fay who kept Lilith safe and so set their own blood to flow in those they gift with insight, foresight and hindsight.

It is we then, who can see beyond, that glimpse the past and present as we walk in ancient places, sensing realities not seen, as we give life to memory in love of myth and legend. We smell them in their divine scent which may well prelude their appearance. We scent their essence in the fragrance of the woods and flowers and sense their touch in the gossamers and winds of the air.

The Fay have their times and places which we may call sacred, and they call home. They have their preferences too, where culture and heritage cross their ways and with whom they feel akin, such are the women of Celtia and men of Slavia, distinct and different peoples with traditions and festivals, strange garbs and fine foods to welcome in the seasons. An inherited respect for things which are both super and natural.

If you cannot see the Fay which I describe, then look to those who have art of word and brush. There are many who paint those sprites and spirits of wood and dell or those who seek metals in the caverns below, and some who favour sweet nectar and flit like butterflies from flower to flower. But I speak of those Lordly Ones of hollow hills and mounds and their rivals the Elven people of the coppice and deep dark wood.

And now I must tell you of the past. These 19th and 20th centuries, these were the times we may call the Celtic twilight. It was then that poets sang again of the Fay, and skilled painters trapped their images to canvas and board. William Blake was such, as was Theodor von Holst and one must always look to Arthur Rackham and perhaps today to sweet Linda Ravenscroft or dear Lynne and Nicola in the ancient place of legend, Tintagel. The visionary artist John Duncan perhaps best captured the character of the Fay. See for instance his picture called the Riding of the Sidhe (pronounced Shee) encapsulating their beauty, richness with power. Now I know this is true, for I was drawn to him and so to them, in the Gardens of Irene.

Come with me in your mind's eye to a small village in the Mediterranean island of Cyprus. You visit a village to see and smell the hills rich with the aroma of thymes and marjorams. The aroma of the old gods rolls down slopes with the spring zephyr to give scent and health to every breath you take.

A willowy European figure flits from square to narrow street, tall and slender, long blonde hair, unlike the locals. In the nearby town, another sunlit day, the same figure appears, slim, sveldt in red dress, but yet again it is the corner of your eye which catches her. Another village, the same fleeting glimpses and then suddenly, as if by magic, she is before you and in conversation. A coincidence?

You do not know how, or why, but you are invited for coffee to her house and her pleasure Garden of Irene, named for the goddess of Peace and Harmony. Her partner talks of botany and the beauty and flora of the island, real things we can see and touch, whilst she talks of Cyprus, the land, and the birth of Aphrodite in the sea foam; her arrival upon a seashell on the rocks near Paphos. You speak of the romance of Berengaria, the fiancée of Richard the Lionheart, the Templars and many mysteries. She speaks of her relationship to John Duncan of whom you had never heard. Amongst the Moroccan scatter cushions and Turkish throws and mused by the lazy smoke of Indian incense, we then talk of essence oils and the Celtic Twilight, of Yeats and Lady Gregory.

Ah yes, I sigh, the Gardens of Irene happened to me. An elegant coincidence with Dierdre, engineered no doubt by those who watch over her from the Crystal Castle and cast a spell on me.

CHAPTER 2

Smok the Dragon

Now that is said and all of what can be traced of how things happen, I can talk and write to you more surely, and move from Crystal Castle, wherever that may be; for in a timeless world it is a small jump to Smok about whom you have to come to learn. And so now we seem to travel North but really, we go East depending from where you happen to start, which means it may be South but never West, for that is where the sun sinks into the sea.

I do wonder if Smok can be considered a fairy, after all he is a dragon and not of this world. I first met him in Glastonbury but as of these days he prefers Tintagel or the hills by Langport way. When his homeland was destroyed by the Black Cross knights, riding screaming winged machines spitting fire and hell, or riding great armoured Leviathans roughshod over farm and field, the people died and had no time for fairy people. Smok's power had long gone and so he wept to see his treasures stripped and taken to the fortress of the Mean Grail and Eagles Nest. His gold was stolen and the livestock taken, people killed without rhyme or reason and the rest enslaved.

Smok came to this Island of the Mighty with some remnants of the White Eagle army who had fought the Black Cross knights. The White Eagle is she who feeds her chicks with her own blood and may sacrifice herself for others, or so says the legend of the Nest. This army first went to Scotland which was not to Smok's taste, as not only was it cold and wet and snowy but many of the natives had difficulty in speaking the same language as everybody else on the big island now called Britain. The local inhabitants insist it is the same language but as all foreigners and visitors to the far northern parts of the great island know, this is not so at all.

For example, there was an important and pleasant city

called Glasgu, meaning in the old tongue, green place, which it was not. It was a land of industry, ships, coal and smoke. The latter he had no problem with, but you had to get about. What finally did it was, when Smok had asked a way from a passing Scots fairy but he never understood a word, despite the fairy translator he had inbuilt into his internal system. The translator said, 'unknown input, error 1707', which he later found out to have been a significant error for some inhabitants. He did however discover there was another domain called Wales, without an h. They had a flag with a dragon on it which sounded auspicious. So off he flew to the south post haste.

He was drawn by instinct I suppose, or magic to a place called Corris. For as he flew a great upside-down whirlwind caught him and threw him down to the ground. And right before him, as he rubbed his eyes, was a woodeny, cabiny, workshop, sort of touristy place called King Arthur's Labyrinth. Dragons get on with Labyrinths. Now it all made sense because dragons and King Arthur had a lot to do with each other too. For in Arthur's time the veil was thin between the worlds of the Fay; the old gods and the new god were in dispute. And he mused and thought, 'wasn't Arthur's surname Pendragon or High Dragon, must be significant'. So, he folded his wings, curled up his tail and put on a happy face and had a look around. Remember he could not be seen except for those with the sight.

Now you may feel, we might have made a jump in time. Time is a feature of fairyland, for it, time, in some ways, does not exist, or at best has relativity to something, 'cos it really is an energy, like a fairy. It used to be straight, travel fast and being linear might have a parallel existence, but, now we know it is curved, or can be, which means in millennia, it can be a circle. What goes around comes around then! depending on how big or small or relative it is. Get it? It does explain what happens next and afterward, or before, when fairies slip in and out of time and place.

Soon he found a pottery shop and a good mortal friend who could make pretend dragons or were they... Well not exactly then, because dragons can be like fairies not only in different places at the same time, but also in different times at the same time. So, he knew what the man would do, and did do, as well as could do. Smok was setting his mind to the future, but being impatient Smok just jumped forward a few years till now. So now, being now, not then, lovely little dragons were being made who puffed harmless wondrous smelling smoke, but no fire. They and the sprites who animated them, were small and happy, content to be seen again as multicoloured beings from another world. So precious were they, they were housed in small cages to keep them safe and secure.

Smok did not see things that way. True they puffed smoke to please their dragon fans and the potter had found a way of making their breath smell of spice and all things nice but Smok was a very big dragon (not anymore but he hadn't got used to being medium) and very old indeed. He didn't like the idea of the cage, but they seemed happy enough. 'It is not that we are kept in,' said one, 'but it keeps mortal, prying fingers out, especially little fingers,' said another.

What Smok really wanted was a dragon master, and these were very few and far between. The dragon Lords, on the other hand, Oberon the King of the Fay, had told him had died out, gone, the last one was seen, indeed, in Arthurs time, in human terms some fifteen hundred years ago. But Smok knew that a dragon master, in his people's dragon language, did not imply suffrage or obedience as to a Lord - no he said to Oberon, 'I need a human who has the mastery of dragon law and can help us dragons survive in the minds of men with our different tribes cultures and ways'.

Now as with all tales of yore one must jump about a bit in our head to understand things, make things add up, look for signs and symbols like + or − in knowledge or even $P(A)$ which by the way is not algebra. Most scientists cannot do this, as academia trains them to be single minded, and hence they are ignorant of life as it is. Great visionary scientists are not that many, but those who study Physics and higher

Maths are not so far from the fairy world, so let us go back a bit and start from where we should have been

Smok had learned by hard experience to adapt. He had started out as normal in the usual way with a diet of maidens and if not around, sheep. He lived in a big cave, at the bottom of a large rocky outcrop of a hill, overlooking a wide meandering river. He did the usual dragon things like collecting gold and twinkling, pretty coloured stones, sitting on them and keeping his tail wrapped around his hoard.

Then that detestable boy decided to end it all. The boy's name was Krak, Krak by name and Krakkers by nature Smok thought. At least he wasn't called George, Smok reminisced, Georges always gave dragons bad vibes. Anyways, Krak had put a big fat juicy sheep right outside the cave entrance. Of course, Smok sniffed, wrinkled his nose and savoured the smell and slid outside to chompse up the delicious morsel. He opened his mouth wide and took up the whole big fat sheep in one great, greedy gulp.

He actually preferred this type of woolly food, some would call mutton, as opposed to lamb which, were as their name implied, much smaller. As for maidens, he thought humans very odd as they gave him slim, skinny bints, with no fat at all. Their idea of what was pretty, or desirable was quite different to Smok's. Looking through the local village at night, when he came out to roam about, whilst peering through windows, he had noticed many lovely, plump, soft, juicy ladies who would make more of a tasty meal. They could keep him well fed, content, happy and going for months. Sheer scale of size and the economy of time made it logical to supply larger ladies. It was always the skinny ones, bony ones, who turned up outside the cave. What dimwit couldn't work out that one good large maiden would cut down on the losses of the smaller ones.

When he did get a thin one, he usually huffed and puffed and told the girl the best thing was to go inside the cave, right to the back, where she could climb up outside and hop it back to the village. They always said they could not as they had been sacrificed to appease Smok, to stop him eating sheep. Seemed a bit warped thinking to him, appeasing him with inedibles didn't match the storyline of pleasing him. So, when dark, in the dead of night, when the village fast asleep, he used to fly off with the maidens and drop them off with the fairies to find them a good home. Usually a godmother turned up to sort it all out as he didn't see himself as a social service.

So back to Krak – the detestable boy, who had, unbeknown to Smok, craftily filled the sheep with sulphur and a bit pf phosphorous for good measure. So Smok took one big, very big gulp.

Baaaang! (that means an echoing bang for being in a cave). There was an enormous explosion of fire, a really big bang! What a roar! Not from Smok, because although he squealed enough to be heard a hundred miles away, the very noisy force of the exploding flames, the big bang, acting like a jet engine threw him back against the cave wall stunning him, whereupon he lost his senses, including the common one. Everything went dark too, for the force of the jet had actually blown the natural dragon fire right out! Smok heard a small, phut and that was it.

Smok could never, ever again, breathe out fire, for once a dragon's pilot flame, deep in a dragon's throat goes out it cannot be relit (matches had not been invented then, you know the ones with long sticks, and later as we shall see or not see, there, was no need to light up due to climate change). True his breath smelt a bit gassier from the unlit pilot light but overall it didn't make too much difference in the general smelly breath of a dragon.

However, that was not the end of the story, for Smok felt his whole mouth was on fire. He had never felt such burning before! The odd accident yes but never this smarting, stinging horrid pain, and the smell of burning, he almost felt sorry for the one or two creatures he had managed to singe or scorch in his lifetime. Still dazed and not thinking straight, he howled loudly and shot up in the sky and then flew straight down, headfirst, into the river, with his mouth wide open. He very nearly drowned, as water and dragons do not mix well and dragons cannot swim. Oh! but the relief of cooling water. It was the steam 'what dunnit' as they say, the steam came out of his nose, mouth ears and stung his eyes, so flapping about and finding it hard to breath and see straight, Smok crawled out onto the bank, flopped down, exhausted by post-traumatic stress and went to sleep.

The villagers were so happy and triumphant that the dragon had gone. They all had a meeting and decided to rename the village from Smokleigh, to Krakow which was a really weird name but that's the way it can be in the fairy world.

CHAPTER 3

Oberon

So how did Smok get to Glastonbury? That is a long story and you have already heard part of it but first we have to realise a change had occurred to Smok, a really Big change, or put another way he had shrunk! Yes, dragons are not meant to get really wet. They really are meant to be dry cleaned. At the very tip of their tail is a little label that clearly says so. They can be licked like cats, or scales slough off like a snake or they can stand in a sand storm to be like 'shot blasted', or in cosmetic terms 'peeled'. All good for being glossy and shiny. Now though, he found himself a big dragon, now at best, well, a medium dragon, about the same size of a common enough mortal size 12, he felt crushed, small, cramped, and paltry. That's me Smok groaned out loud, poultry, no better than a turkey!

Oberon who happened to have heard the roar when a hundred miles away, turned up and took pity on the bedraggled dragon. Oberon looked him over just at the moment Smok had likened himself to a turkey.

Now you might well ask why Oberon, King of the Fay of the West, had turned up here on the banks of a mighty river in the middle of the endless Land of Fields. It would have been better if you had not asked for then I would not have had to answer such an interrupting awkward question. The thing is, he had a penchant, that's right, for water fairies and this was the best place for them. All these long rivers flowing slowly were great places for secret assignations. They were so common that the big city where Vars and Sava lived (you need not know about them) had a river mermaid complete with shield and buckler as their emblem, protectoress. The city is 400 miles from the cold cobalt blue sea so that tells you the mer and water fairies' range inland a very long way. The little lady who Oberon was meeting was named Ariel, which is quite another story.

Oberon is not such a bad chap. They were not friends, he and Smok, as Oberon, by nature being a king only felt he should have subjects. It wasn't as though Oberon was shy, but he tended to be aloof. He did admire himself a lot, so tended to mix with those who admired his physique. One of his closest admirers was his masseuse who kept Oberon looking shiny and well oiled, glossy, sleek and smoothed and his hairdresser who was particularly good at a cut that showed off his power horns. But Oberon found the right words for Smok.

'Not poultry Smok', said Oberon 'you mean small paltry. You have spelt it wrong in your head. You are not a turkey, which after all, is rather a striking bird. You meant paltry meaning small, meagre, trifling, insignificant, negligible, inadequate, insufficient, scant, scanty, derisory, pitiful, pitiable, pathetic, miserable, sorry, wretched, puny. Isn't that right?

'Yes, that me. O woe is me' mumbled Smok who sighed and sighed again.

Oberon raised himself to his full height and towered over the dragon. Realising this was not tactful at that precise moment, he came back down but kept the towering voice all the same. No you are not paltry dear dragon but petite, unpretentious, free spirited, generous of spirit, good-looking, comely, fair, handsome, graceful, exquisite, gorgeous, refined, delicate, cute, divine, blooming, rosy, bonny, beauteous, statuesque, Junoesque, pulchritudinous, well-favoured, bewitching, enchanting, appealing, ravishing, personable, pleasing, fetching, winning, alluring, and in your own way, rather grand'. This mollified Smok somewhat who said, 'Am I really pulchritudinous, you are so kind.'

As you see one of the characteristics of the King of the Fairies is to go on a bit. But there was another problem, that unfortunately, without thinking, because he was still examining his vocabulary, to see if he had any more adjectives to tell Smok, Oberon went on to say… 'I just love your new tie dye look'

'What, what, what the hell'! Smok looked at himself in the water and it was true, all the colours had run in the first water wash he had ever gotten in to! Gone was his lovely red head set and russet neck, his green blue wings had yellow streaks, he was washed up or in or out, but he was not his singular coloured self.

Seeing his mistake and the look of horror on Smok's face, Oberon smoothly and suavely went on to say. 'Smok, you old trend setter who would have thought that you would become a fashion icon – a fashionista, well done – I shall make sure you have a feature in the Fairy Style next issue, you might even make it into Cosmo'.

And now you know why all the dragons in Corris have such multicolours who run and combine to give a lovely sheen and why nearly all fashion dragons are now multicoloured thanks to Smok – well no, Krak actually if you know the whole story.

Oberon also fixed it into the minds of men to put up a commemorative statue to Smok by his old lair. To amuse himself Oberon made sure that the image of Smok every now and again spouted fire and roared. This especially amused Oberon as his piece de resistance. When the dragon flamed and roared, unsuspecting tourists having their photo taken, jump for their lives and so being around Smok became fun which all fairies love.

Smok was still not well or himself and he had not eaten for days. If you think about it, he had never had to fend for himself, as someone had always turned up with a meal. And now no fire and no fire meant no barbecue. 'What do I do Oberon,' he pleaded, 'what am I to eat'?

'In Wales don't try and eat sheep they have better things to do with them in Wales than feed dragons.'

'And where or what is Wales said Smok?'

'You need not worry about that yet. You will get there in time (remember time switching?) and after all despite the spices you have just had a good meal which can last a dragon a century sometimes. Now, the only answer long term, is to turn vegetarian a bit like us, for we feed on all manner of sweet things but mostly nectar, honey and dew. You know, all the sorts of airy-fairy stuff we can eat but not, I agree the best for sickly dragons.

Ah I have it! Apples; an apple a day keeps the doctor away, so in your case that's good. You will not be far from Hereford so maybe you could settle there. Ummm but its best to have some cheese with apple and Hereford's not the place for that. I have it, its Somerset for you my lad. You need a good Somerset Ploughman's lunch every day. A girt lump of Cheddar cheese, a pickled onion and Branston pickle, to give you a fiery feeling in the tum and a hunk of wholemeal spelt bread from Burns the Bread with a good swig of Hecks cider. I am talking Avalon man! Well in your case, dragon!'

'I love the idea of Avalon' said Smok. 'Are you sure about the vegetarian bit? I have never heard of a vegetarian dragon in the histories.

'But that's it old chum – I am making you the fashion leader, the icon, a fashionista, the celeb everyone wants to meet or find. They even have a cave you could squat in for a while. Gwyn keeps his hounds there, so it can be a bit smelly and noisy when they howl to scare the natives. It's cool man, dragon, or in your case warm! You got witches, fairies, wizards, neo-liberals, Vikings, Catholics, Protestants, charmers, occultists, goblins and piskies up from Cornwall, knights and ladies, ancient Egyptian princesses, goddesses so no one is going to be freaked by a dragon; you will love it. They will call the place Glastonbury those days.

I will introduce you to Ashling, for she of the Fay looks out for Somerset, right up as far the dragon chalk hills. Such is her domain and she especially looks after apples. Come on no time to lose, let's get you hunkered down for a nice long dragon sleep. In time I will make the introduction. Take a leaf out of my book – go for it dragon.' Oberon sung a sweet lullaby and Smok went to sleep for ages.

Oberon placed him gently in a cave in the Owl mountains where the dragon snored gently for a very long,

long, time, for a good Madras curry can do that and what Smok had eaten was the modern equivalent. When he did wake up in bad times and how he got to Avalon will have to wait for there is much more to say about the 7th court of the Fairies of the West. As for Smok there is more to tell so you will have to wait.

And that we might say is the character of Oberon. He can be compassionate but likes to laugh and can play jokes but is sure of himself, liking his own way and getting by magic what he wants.

CHAPTER 4

Titania

It was one of those November days when the clouds were a sheet of dull grey. The English Channel sent its waves rolling up the sloping shingle beach with a tumble of foam before hissing back to the grey green sea.

Tom was beach combing. He walked along the edge of the wave line, occasionally dodging the seventh wave which always ran further up the beach. He was looking for the occasional semi-precious stones that hid amongst the myriad ordinary pebbles. It was best to do this on a sunny day, when the sparkle stood out from the mundane but who can order the weather, unless one was a witch.

But then he reasoned Brighton had its fair share of witches and fairies. He knew one middle aged woman who called herself Drusilla. Tom reckoned she was probably named Cheryl or something in real life. She dressed in black and used a bit of 'Goth' makeup yet favoured pink hair. Anyway, 'whatever keeps you happy' he spoke to the breeze.

In his mid-twenties Tom had taken to wearing a beard. It was fashionable nowadays and being of that late millennial generation, he was basically lazy, so had stopped shaving, and then as luck would have it many others had the same lazy idea brought about by a school system that did not encourage a work ethic. Hence as his grandfather kept saying he was a perennial student. Not work shy but he didn't know what to do with life and if you played it right, the Social would look after you.

Then he saw the pebble. Rounded and rubbed by the sea into a tiny pebble it was a dull olive green which had rolled all the way from the Western sea. He knew it straight away as piece of Olivine and when polished, would be a nice peridot. Tom had been tumbling pebbles to polish them since he was a kid and had quite a collection at home from white quartz, common at Brighton, to amethysts and even garnet. Now a green peridot, the fairy colour. The birthstone of Libra.

He had reached the skeleton of the old West pier ravaged by fire and then swept away by storms and gales. The old pier meant nothing to him, a bygone time, as the monumental i360 viewing tower stood over him, a statement to the new world leaving the past to wash away.

He looked up and spoke to the sky, as one does, "Ah little pebble how small you are but packed with energy. I wonder if you have more in you than that monster tower behind me. I mean, are your little atoms more powerful than a manmade concrete edifice"? He began to hum a little ditty grandad had taught him. 'Little pebble upon the sand, now your lying here in my hand', he kissed the pebble for some reason and wished that he knew the story behind where the little gem had come from – it was a big mistake – anyone could have made the same error.

The world exploded around him in a whirl of vibrating colours and a great wailing shriek filled his ears and stunned him to numbness, leaving him dumbfounded and staring at a half-naked woman with horns curling through her red hair and with what appeared to be shimmering wings attached to her. In fact, the woman seemed to shimmer and certainly shiver as she crossed her arms and tried to stop her teeth chattering.

'Who on earth are you?' she said, 'and what miserable month is this?'

'November miss,' Tom replied.

'November', she shouted, 'November, I don't do November, how dare you bring me here in November! I come with the summer not November. You must have read about me in those silly plays the Upstart Crow wrote. Midsummer is my time not November. Shut up, don't talk, I must get some clothes on.' And so the apparition spun round and transformed into a lady in full evening dress with a faux fur wrap. 'That's better,' she said whilst looking Tom up and down as though he was a distasteful worm.

Having gathered some but not all his wits Tom gathered some courage too and said, 'to answer the first part of your question, my name is Tom Ogden and who are you?'

'First of all, young man, you speak when I tell you too and not one before, Un-der-stood?'.

'But you asked me the question', but he got no further for she yelled at him in no uncertain manner whilst holding up an imperious hand, 'Shut up until I tell you to speak Tom Oak Valley for that is your proper name. And I fail to understand why you do not recognise me. Everyone knows me; I am Titania, Queen of the Fairies and no jokes from you about my beautiful curves. It was the upstart crow who gave me that silly Greek name as he did with my consort Oberon that good for nothing nimby fairy. You may call me Majesty.'

'But Majesty, I don't believe in fairies,' he got no further.

'You don't believe in fairies! I don't believe it! How can you not believe in fairies? Isn't this Brighton, it is full of fairies, everywhere has fairies. Who do you think looks after nature if not fairies? What! You just think sprinkling a bit of water and fertilizer on a plant is looking after nature – how stupid. You have a lot to learn young man.'

'I may have,' he re-joined and being somewhat more relaxed in these very odd circumstances he chanced a question. 'Why does a pretty woman like you have horns growing out of your head?'

'How dare you speak to me in such a tone you moron, you worm, you, despicable toad. Pretty woman indeed! I am a queen of beauty the most desirable and beauteous creature you are ever likely to meet in your whole life toad. Pretty isn't even half way toad.'

'Well blow me if I have not upset her precious majesty,' Tom retorted. Whereupon she pursed her lips, puffed her cheeks and blew at him. Tom was literally blown off his feet. 'You get what you ask Tom Toad,' she said standing over him.

'I am not a toad Tom shouted back,' for Tom thought

toads either ugly or vacuous like the Toad of Toad Hall about whom he had learned due to his grandfather reading to him at bedtime from a book called Wind in the Willows.

Titania smiled ever so sweetly and from nowhere a wand appeared in her hand. He lay flat on his back still looking up at her. 'Horns my dear are a universal symbol of power even strength. They have more meaning than gold crowns and show that we of the fay can do things mankind cannot'. She leant forward and touched Tom's chest.

Tom felt an ice-cold shaft penetrate him and he began to shrink, he watched his legs thin, his hands seemed to implode and then it all went dark. It was as though he was in a stifling bundle of material stuff, the light was blotted out. He struggled up a long tunnel and suddenly he emerged back into daylight and found himself looking up at the Fairy Queen who now seemed much taller than before, in fact, when he thought about it, he was looking at the toe of an elegant court shoe and lovely shaped ankle. He looked back at the tunnel he had come from and with ultimate horror and gripping fear, he realised it was his own trouser leg he had crawled through. He looked at his arms and legs, now all knobbly and rough with warts and coloured a dull olive green. He was a toad. He shouted up at her, 'Get me out of here, I am sorry, I speak too much,' but he realised it was not happening for he heard instead of words a limp cross between a burp and a croak.

'Ah ha,' Titania said, 'I see my toad has emerged. The beach is no place to be toad'. She turned back into the first fairy form Tom had seen. She picked him up and placed him carefully (for which he was thankful) into a pouch at her belt. He felt them lift high into the sky and then because it was cold he fell asleep.

Being a toad was not the best experience of Tom's life even though Her Majesty gave him a little red velvet jacket to wear and held him, when at the fairy court, at her heel with a golden chain and collar. At night he slept on a beautiful blue soft as thistle down cushion at Her Majesties feet. He enjoyed the dancing and the music and watching the strange rainbow creatures of the magic world. In fact, he was quite happy doing nothing which was what he usually did anyway. Occasionally he was sent out to arrest snails and slugs who overstepped the mark and ate too many leaves which the fairies had painted, other than that he enjoyed the eternal warmth and happiness of the place. He did however grow fatter and although as we know he was lazy, he did eventually get bored and wanted to go home.

He spoke with the Fairy Ashling who looked after the apples and told him that if he had been a prince in disguise someone would kiss him and all would be well. No chance there then Tom Oak Valley.

When he was transported or as he called it in his mind, when he was beamed up, he was still clutching at his olivine peridot pebble. He had kept it under his blue cushion; it sort of reminded him of where he belonged.

One day when Titania was having her 'hair done' he got it out to see if he could juggle.

Her Majesty screamed, she screeched, she roared, 'Where did you get that jewel toad?'

'When I first met you Majesty on the beach at Brighton,' toad replied. 'I kissed it and you appeared'.

'Well of course I did, silly toad, stupid boy, it's one of my summoning stones. Why didn't you tell me you had it awful toad?'

'You never asked Majesty, when you arrived, you were too busy being bossy,' toad responded and with some gusto blurted out in fairy speech (which all fairies understand whatever their tribe) you rudely told me to shut up, so I did.'

'Oh foolish toad, you have been here too long away with you.' She pulled out her wand, the one with the star thing on the end, not her best one, which had crystal. Pointing it at him she began to make a spell. 'Where was it you said you came from toad, Brighthelmstone?'

'No, no,' toad shouted, 'that is the old name from the Prince Regent's day, I was in Brighton, by the West Pier'.

Of course, it was his error, for the West Pier was no more and Fairy Queens are pretty thoughtless.

He woke up on the beach underneath the West Pier. The year was as he later discovered 1954. At that time the pier was lit up at night and attracted a much more select clientele than the down-market Palace Pier down the other end near the cockle and whelk stalls. And since that fateful day, over the years, many locals and visitors have seen him beach combing looking for an elusive green pebble. In fact, he taught his son, and grandchildren and even great grandchildren to beach comb for pebbles. Young Tom, his grandson, the lazy one is proving to be the best ever at beach combing and he likes to spend time east of the old West pier. He got to grow up a bit fairyfied because his grandfather read him Wind in the Willows every night at bedtime.

CHAPTER 5

Ashling

It was Oberon himself who deigned to visit me in Avalon. Bringing along with him a small dragon with a nice personality called Smok. I thought it a name short for something but that was all there was. Dragons usually have long names or be the dragon of something such as the dragon of Wales or the dragon of Somerset, but this guy was just Smok.

Bit poorly in spirit when I first met him, but he soon cheered up for I fed him Ashmead's Kernel apples, the best tasting russet apple known to man. Ugly to look at nutty to eat. He was soon a regular, although not really there from a human perspective at the Who'd a Thought It pub, he liked the size of the cheese portions in the ploughman's special. I used to dress him as a mortal by my power of shaping but unfortunately his breath was not the sweetest and when mixed with rich cheddar – well! So he was on his own a lot.

When it came to May and the locals ran up and down the High Street supporting long big red and white dragons, he got very excited and flapped up and down the street after them creating a wind to keep the people cool, as it is hot work carrying bits of dragon around.

Some of the lads from Minehead and Padstow thought this was a bit wet of the Glaston crew as carrying the 'oss' as they do, means that you should carry till you are about to drop. Anyway, someone told Smok that these 'oss's were sort of dragon like and off he went to Cornwall leaving me to do all the work for he had been helping me keep the fairies in hand and at work looking after the blooms. For if the apple tree does not bloom then no apples come.

The trouble with my job, which is organising the tree fairies, is that fairies are basically unreliable except of course for me. I am, in my opinion, very reliable. Fairies too do not always like heights and generally tees are well, high. Another problem I have is that trees are well, very wooden.

Inevitably the trees are slow and rooted firmly in a self-belief in their own superiority. They get very old and tetchy, throwing bits of themselves at the wind when it upsets them and when in a real tantrum, they just throw themselves on the ground in temper.

This last strategy of course doesn't help them at all, as they cannot get back up, so they have to come down to earth or reality, with a crash bang! Some of the tall ones do really get above themselves especially the fir trees. In a mixed woodland they often stand out above the others. Look at me they shout, see how tall I am compared to you, fat oaks, or spindly birches all pale and wan. Of course, the others get their own back when they get ready to sleep through winter. It's my team who paint the leaves in beautiful oranges, yellows and browns leaving the others for ever green, or even bluish but however hard they try they cannot make the glory of normal trees in autumn, or when we dress the trees in Spring with a multitude of pretty flowers.

Anyway, my favourite tree is the apple. Every Spring we make them sparkle with blossom in pinks and white that billow in the breeze as bees buzz from tree to tree. Next, as summer grows, they become heavy with delicious fruits of reds and yellows, green and russet. Some apples are sweet, others tart or even sour, but always health giving and useful to men and their ways. We the Fay, taught men how to cultivate apples and give varieties that serve different purposes.

In the land of the Saxon, Angle and Jute folk I settled down in the island of apples men call Avalon. This was after I left my home in the Middle East which was too hot for me in the summer. I got a lift on a boat with a man called Aeneas after great Troy had fallen. I could never have flown this far against the winds blowing from the great ocean in the West. After arriving at Totnes and after the trouble with the giants thereabouts, I flew up country to the summer country where I still have my home.

From a fairy perspective men and women can be a bit weird around trees. From time to time they hug them not realising as I said earlier, trees are well, wooden. By the time the tree knows it has been hugged the person will have passed to the other side.

Then there is Jack. Now Jack in the Green is a male tree sprite who has a habit of manifesting himself like a green man in the month of May. He runs about in the woods like a shadow, frightening young girls if he can and if they are willing he might take one to his bower, where bliss overtakes them both. Trouble is men nowadays pretend to be him, dressing up in costumes made of rags and stuff to look like leaves and then all manner of things may happen, especially if the Lord of Misrule appears.

My problem comes with the autumn and winter with the cider drinkers. It's easier to see us fay folk when the leaves are gone. So, the cider drinkers, who by the way, see a lot of things which are not there at all, convince themselves that spirits live in the trees and spirits like fireworks. I have no idea where they get this from but there is 'nowt as queer as folks.' These men and yes women and children go about Wassailing and this means hooting loudly and shooting shotguns up into the trees, singing songs and as usual, with cider, which we all know addles the brain, getting people drunk.

All this noise is frightening to us fairies and sometimes with the shooting of shotguns the pellets can make holes in our wings! I make sure I am sitting on a wide branch, else wings are not the only things that get a pellet. Of course, we can catch the pellets and we sometimes throw them back which men call accidental ricochets.

It is in the deep mid-winter that I travel East to where we gather in the hollow hills, by the great white horse. Deep underground in the warmth of the fairy blacksmiths forge, the embers shield us from winters thrall; we dream till Spring.

Which is when Jezebel Velvet struck. She was 16 years old and thought everyone stupid, especially her parents. She never bothered to speak to people but just glowered at them from under her purple hair. Already she had a couple of piercings. The first was the belly button so mum wouldn't see and then, when a year older, the left nostril. As you would expect there was a screaming fit, no not from mum and dad but from Jez who reacted to what dad said. He thought she should get a chain attached so he could lead her to do some homework. Stupid joke.

Next came the tattoo. Same strategy, placed just above the knicker line and admired by all her friends on Facebook with loads of shares. Some of the pervs in class wanted to pay to touch it! Was she that daft? No way.

Today she was going to the abbey orchard baiting tourists. She liked to be rude and tell them how stupid they were to do all this Arthur stuff. Sometimes she said she was a witch and enjoyed the feeling of power when some believed her, especially if she had her black and red clothes on.

Today she kept to the shadow of the trees. Today was boy bait day. She would pick a likely looking geek and say 'Wanna Velcro'. They would clear off pretty quick which made her laugh and reinforced her sense of being different and superior to mere ordinary mortals. After all she was hailed by mum and dad as super clever and bound to be the first in the family to go to university.

Her parents said she was shy. They made excuses for her behaviour not knowing what to do with a teenager except dock pocket money, which she soon got around by talking about her human rights and child abuse.

Two young children, pretending to be fairies, spotted her and ran over to the tree she was under. They were girls aged about seven and wearing fairy dresses and wings. 'we are fairies they chorused.

Go way you f*****g excrescences she yelled. There are no fairies stupid and you look silly dressed up like sugar plums, stupid gits. Don't your mum tell you such stories are for kids, they are not real so p**s off'.

Sitting above Jezebel was Ashling the chief tree fairy.

She was pretty annoyed at Jezebel's crude and rude behaviour especially as one of the little girls had started to cry. Choosing a big apple she dropped it straight onto Jezebel Velvets head. (that was not her real name but her avatar). A thud, then an 'ouch' ensued.

Surprised and a little stunned Jezebel shouted at the tree, 'stupid tree who do you think I am, f****g Isaac Newton?' She then kicked the tree with her big boots - big mistake.

Ashling dropped from the tree and confronted Jezebel. 'What a selfish little madam you are. Ignorant too, excrescences indeed. Who do you think you are the Queen of the May? I bet you can't spell excrescences.' As a matter of fact, Jezebel could and knew what it meant too, only she had her mouth open at this moment and so was speechless.

'I am the fairy Ashling and I am going to teach you a lesson and as you can now see fairies do exist! Never kick a tree for as you see, the bark is bruised just like you.' Whereupon Ashling kicked Jezebel hard on the shin.

'Ouch, s**t,' exclaimed Jezebel, 'that hurt you are a real dickweed, hoser.'

'Takes one to know one,' Ashling retorted and promptly stuck an apple in Jezebel's mouth.

Ashling twirled and whirled, weaving and spinning gossamer threads around Jezebel pinning her to the tree like the way you may have seen it done in bad cowboy films.

'I cannot breathe, Jezebel sent the message from her brain, because she really knew fairies could read your mind and anyway, she had an apple in her mouth.

'Yes you can, through your nose, which is by the way, unhappy about having a hole stuck in it and what looks like a curtain ring shoved in it and it's not even gold.' That was all the sympathy she got.

The hours passed, the abbey gates closed, and the evening chill crept into Jezebel's body. 'Mum and dad will get really worried if I am not back soon,' she said to no one having chewed her way through the apple, which was quite sweet. Darkness came.

At home mum and dad had indeed become worried, very

worried. They rang round her friends who had no news except for Mrs. Jones who said she had guests in her b&b who had mentioned an abusive girl in the orchard at the abbey. Dad decided to go look for Jezebel. After walking the streets and talking to a few people in the pubs, where she should never have gone but did, and so with no success he climbed over the abbey railings, calling Jezebel's name, which for the true record was Angelica, poor girl.

Startled by her dad's voice, she woke up suddenly, freezing cold and feeling odd. She rubbed the bump on her head. She was not tied up and thought she must be dreaming. She saw the very big apple on the ground beside her, the one that landed on her head and she picked it up. It winked at her! Double take. It winked again.

"'Dad I am so sorry,' she said as she hugged the big masculine lump she was familiar with, recognising the love that flowed into her and feeling his relief.

'Well that's a phrase I haven't heard in a long time,' he said.

'I'm sorry dad not just for this but I think I fell asleep as simple as that. Awful excuse I know but what else can I say'. She smiled at the apple and felt a gentle kiss on her cheek and she could have sworn she saw a pale figure flit among the trees. She knew now for certain what she saw was no moth!

CHAPTER 6

Finola

On the whole Fairies are not the most reliable or trustworthy of folk. That certainly can be said of humans too, for legend has it that the fairies only faded from sight when betrayed by humans at the time the Golden Strangers came to the shores of these Islands at the end of the World.

These men and sassy women with their blonde and red hair, their iron long swords and heavy shields soon killed off the dark folk, banishing them to the outerlands and dark forests. The magic of the dark folk was no match for the Golden Strangers who hunted them down and took their heads, till there were no more. And so, the fairies were left friendless for the small dark ones were the fairies' friends.

The new people hated the Fay, for they feared them. They could not penetrate the strong magic of the Fay who would not allow themselves to be seen. They could however be heard and their songs and whispers in the dark at night struck strange fears in the Strangers minds and sent shivers to their spine. The Strangers set their dogs toward the sounds, but they just cringed and whined and slunk by the wall.

Fairies always lamented the passing of mortals to another place and regretted their mouldering in the earth or the burnings that turned them to ash. The immortal fairies had passed to women the art of healing with herbs and potions. For healing herbs are always close by the paths and tracks of fairies; best seen when the dew is heavy on the ground as faint trails through grass, or the bending of leaf stalks as though some breeze had passed that way.

The higher of the Fay always knew when mortal passing was near. Not the passing of an accident or war but the lingering, the flickering when the life force was fading and moving from the human flesh that had held it so long. It was a seeping; a lessening of mind and body and the Fay knew when the end was due.

To harry and punish these Strangers the Fay decided to prey upon their superstition, teach them lessons of humility. Big, lumbering mortals, they were, so cock sure, sporting their arm rings, torcs, bangles and dressing their golden braids with ribbon, the Fay would mock them. For the Strangers had two things in common with the Fay and that was the love of jewellery and fine clothes. Both disliked black, a mournful colour.

So it was, that at the time of passing the Fay would ask one of the lesser fairies, one of the goblin tribe to shriek outside the house of the passenger. She would keen and moan, as though in pain, just like the cold North wind that howls loud and sends sighing drafts of cold that makes the spine shiver. The Strangers cowered inside their homes and held hands, close to the fire knowing the time of departure was nigh. The windows would rattle and the doors creak and something scuttled across the floor. It was not a nice trick to play but the Fay remembered the small dark ones who had been their friends.

The Strangers in their tongue said this was indeed the banshee a woman of the fairy mound and they knew it was an impending doom that gave them fear of the sort they had wrought on others.

When first they had come with silver words that shone with lies and deceit, they had glimpses of the Fay and it was then that Finola was glimpsed by Fionn the warrior. She had knelt to close the eyes of her friend, the small dark lad with the shining eyes. It was he, the lad, who had given her the small tortoise shell butterfly with the ragged wings to heal. He had pleaded with her to give the fragile creature life again and she had done so. Her breath had set the butterfly on its way to find the warmth of sun and restore its lightness and battered beauty.

She had knelt down to close the lad's lifeless eyes when the warrior struck. Fairies feel no need for physical hurt or pain for their hurt is of the spirit and the senses, six in all. The iron sword slashed into her calf causing a burning she had never known. For a second, she was dissolved into a thousand shining particles of diamond light and her mind for a second departed into a grey light that held no pictures. And this she felt was like a mortal pain and her leg no longer took her weight, she was lame and damaged. She flew high into the sky amongst the small creatures who live upon the wind. She looked beauteous in the starry sky and her wings gave Silverlight to bats and moths and birds that flock and fly by night.

Fionn leapt back, for the dark-haired beauty he had seen had vanished from his sight. Now he was blinded by a great light of a thousand diamonds that stole his consciousness. His great sword fell to the earth, his buckler now heavy, dragged him to the bloodied sward. And so, he lay blinded and unconscious till the crescent moon arose.

At this time the elven folk, no friend of the Fay, stole from the wood, with their darts and blowpipes ready and they stole away the bodies of the fallen dark folk as if by magic and no trace of them were found when the Strangers came to take the heads.

It is Finola and her handmaids who paint the wings of butterflies, concealing moths, gilding and shining the backs of the six-legged tribes that crawl and swim and fly. It is she who guards them and hides them in winter cold and finds them food amongst the weeds and crops, for all the mortal world lives upon each other, passing and then coming yet again. Finola holds to that spirit of empathy and sympathy for the small and less significant, for the harmed and damaged beings who struggle to survive the turning of the years wheel.

So her pain was acute, for she could not walk as before, as fairies cannot heal each other for their magic is one of service to other kind. Time heals or changes all and her knowledge gave comfort as she soared into the night sky.

Looking down from on high she saw that Fionn was recovering from his shock and blow. He stumbled as a blind man and had been left for dead. She saw that he was comely and well-muscled and without the paint that some men prick into their skin when young and foolish and when old, looks shrivelled and the mighty images hang dry, limp and forlorn telling of the decay of the body. She disdained such crudity of maiming the soft mortal flesh.

She touched his arm to lead him straight and he flinched and called in fright as to who touched him. He begged for mercy or a sword with which to fight. She asked him which was best, and he said a sword. 'What a foolish man you are,' she said, 'a boy in a grown body but a mind of a child like so many of you strangers, a bully with no brain for what would you do with your sword? Slash the air? Poke the soil? It would not hold your weight if you lent upon it. You are blind to see and blind of brain.'

Who are you? Fionn called out angrily.

'I am Finola the Fairy woman you cut with a sword so that I would fall, and you could ravish me with ease before my throat was slit, for you are barbarian and made bloodthirsty by your so called magic practicing priests of the oak and mistletoe. For they have no magic and cannot write, for fear someone else may take their power. But you who cannot see, I feel may change some ways. For I see your wife is seeking you amongst the dead and she mourns you as a true lover should. Come I shall steal you away and make you my own for a year and a day and make you my lover to caress and heal me or my spirit despite my wound.'

Fionn had no power as Finola took his arm and led him to the island that floats in the world sea. Here they sang and danced in the air and he came to love Finola for she fed him, and that is much of what a warrior needs, and why mortal men love women. She danced with him and loved him till he was spent and wretched, but all the time he could not see but his wits were sharpened none the less.

It came to be his last day of his capture. Finola had let him touch the softness of the rabbit skin, the breath of a butterfly, the sweet smell of hyacinth and the beauty of silken garb. He had become a person of his senses, his anger was gone, his sense of justice gained.

'These sentiments are not gifting from me,' she said, 'but

what manhood truly is, the maturity of mind over body. It is not the taking but the generosity of giving, which is the sign of greatness. You the Golden Strangers have destroyed what was good and war has become your world's way. You have found in yourself this past year and one today, things of wonder which you did not understand and have learned without sight, to question and test out what you are told. So, come with me and I will return your sight.'

She guided him to a wild running stream and there was beneath the run a wide pool. 'Look into the pool.' she said.

'I cannot,' he replied.

'If that is so then what is that?'

He gasped for he saw reflected the dark-haired beauty of Finola smiling at him as he leaned staring into the pool. Then he saw an enormous salmon the size of which would fill a man's belly for many days. He had heard from the Druids of the salmon of wisdom which, if a man ate of it, he would be the wisest of all. Finola laid a fishing spear by his side.

Fionn paused and he saw the beauty of the fish as the sun caught its markings. Indeed, it was a great fish, but he was well fed, he had no need for food. He reached to the water for many things were as yet unreal and the fish swam to his finger and touched it. The whole scene and feeling was just beautiful, fulfilling and satisfying. Fionn turned around and Finola smiled, 'truly you now have learned the wisdom of the senses.'

'I have', he said, 'but I will have to make up some tall tale to tell my tribe and the druids for otherwise no one will believe my change of mind and heart. I must thank you for your restoring my sight.'

'You never lost it but momentarily, for there are none so blind as those who believe they cannot see. For blindness comes both with and without belief and often the children of men are blind to reality choosing only what they want to see.'

And so the story of Fionn was woven with fairy thread and tales were told of his might beyond this mortal world.

Finola with her gift of foresight had seen that Fionn changed the Golden Strangers and their savagery. Such brutality lessened as his warrior band of young men, the Fianna, became legendary for their generosity in goods, trade and even battle. She saw the Romans come and the end of the Druids. But still men fight and hanker after war and a new warlike priesthood preached the need for blood to end any argument.

Today more than ever before she is needed to tend the small and beautiful harmony of the kingdom that is Mother Earth for mortals and another place just out of sight which is only seen by those who wish the cunning of the ancient ways. The folk sing like the Fay of change and the sadness of the passing of so much good.

CHAPTER 7

Mabh

Mabh was never slow in coming forward except in early mornings. In the evening she was always languorous, laid back and sometimes sultry, sexy, depending on the mood of the setting sun. But mornings were always bad.

She was a water fairy of the type men love to fear and in turn, are ready to be seduced, devoured by her bold advances. She was friends with the Mer people although they favoured salted water but would still swim the rivers whilst she and her kind had need unsalted and did not go to sea. The Mer gave her gifts pearls and cowrie shells, and her favourite magic amber which warmed to her breast when she rubbed it to her skin and they made combs for her to smooth her heavy tresses.

Mabh was not bad in the sense of wickedness but she was a challenge, as she chose to use her powers to be seen by many folk. She gained some sense and feeling of power when men admired her body and felt pleased that women looked askance at her curves and graces with envious eyes or even jealous ones. It simply pleased her, and pleasure is a trait of any fairy. She also knew that power corrupts so she was careful in her ways for she was not corrupt, meaning a willingness to act dishonestly in return for personal gain except sometimes in matters of the heart and desire which gained her disapproval from the Fairy Court. But she could live with that.

Water is a common substance and so often ignored. It has many moods and faces. It is of the air yet falls to ground, and when the earth is swollen it comes forth to nourish and sustain all living things. It was from her waters that Mabh had learned so many artful tricks of colour, form and mood.

She was not a native of these flat, green lands of willow and fragrant meadowsweet, although her favourite haunts had always been where wide rivers flooded over banks to feed the soil. She had known the Great Queen who had seen her through the perfumed smoke as though a god. Yet she was not such as those of the mighty spirit realm, where Princes of land and sea have their courts in cloud or mountain top. No, she was of the otherworld, the Land of Fay, which exists like an island far out to sea or in the great sea of stars above.

It was with the Great Queen she shared the art of glamour and transformation. It was here that she learned to be, and not yet to be, to appear and disappear, or as another, to confuse and tease and look like, but not be alike, and to have what one may will by garb stealth, the art of dressing for a purpose. It was she Mabh, who taught Merlin his tricks of deception and shape shifting which birthed the once and future king men call, Arthur causing great distress and hurt to the wife and daughters of the Prince of Kernow. She did not see this coming, or feel responsible, 'for like water, life,' she said, 'is fluid with unforeseen results'. That is the way with Mabh.

As for Merlin who abused her trust, she placed a glamour upon him that he could not break which amused her greatly and she often stared at him within the great oak which held him fast and he glared back. But when he smiled knowingly, she felt disturbed, because he was, after all a wizard. They had much in common and were friendly in their own special way, yet as rivals.

So Mabh it was that passed on her Eastern ways to the women of the North, for she taught the whiles and use of clays and colours, of oils and unguents and the use of herbs and sweet smelling perfumes to create allure, reveal beauty and entice men to their doom like moths to candle flame, whatever women decide should be the outcome. Her water fairies became adept at change and disguise, the slow art of love where waters run dark and dangerous, the love making of the storm that rages and casts aside all obstacles. Sweet words of nothingness and flirtation with purpose, words that simply make life sweet, poems that give worth and wit.

Her greatest art was that of the language of eye talk. She

would appear as some illusive glance, hard to see, a glance a smile that had a hint – a hint of what? That was her art, impossible to explain an impish glint of fantasies or rapture, all beyond human understanding or wisdom. She and her fairy type fed upon the power her eyes gave her, as did the emotion of the consequence and anguish of the injured. Not so nice for the victim caught in a web or caught in the weeds of the river of emotion that can drag you down to the depths of despair. 'Don't go in the water if you cannot swim, and don't get of your depth,' and in truth, both fair warnings.

Mabh was also a lover of costume. True hers was a body beautiful, and her wings a gossamer of light, but she knew well the art of costume. For she loved silken stockings of white and black and even ones with rings of black and white. A Basque of black, with a small dash of red and a barely concealing black laced mask, would make her belle of the Fairy Ball each year without fail. However gorgeous the others may be in damask and satin, or wool and fine hair fabrics, ornamented with gold and silver thread she had learned from the Queen of the South that less is always more.

So, in your, the readers time, it came about that Ellie decided it was her time to do something about Thomas. He was the most desirable bloke about. Not good looking but polite which was a rare commodity in the 21st century, and he had manners, yes real manners and actually said please and thank you! Intelligent, well he read the Daily Mail so some questions, but he played rugby not football so a bit more up market than football she thought. He supported Cornish Pirates rather than Bath, so he liked underdogs she guessed, and probably animals – nice boy.

Of course, his view on the Pirates had been told her on the first ever game she attended. Apparently, they would never really get up the league because Exeter Chiefs in the proper big boys league always stole away their best players. She persevered and stood in cold muddy fields and progressed to making hot drinks and joined other wives and girlfriends in club duties but not a glimmer of interest came from Thomas, just camaraderie at work and play.

But then came the club Midsummer Ball right down in far magical Penzance.

On the night of the full moon at midnight she stole outdoors naked as the day she was born. She shivered as it was cold, and she was excited. She had taken a mirror from her dressing table and now set it upon the garden bench whilst she kneeled in front of it. She lit a red candle placing it between her and the mirror. Nothing happened. Someone at the Fragrant Earth shop in Glastonbury had told her that fairies like fragrance and she had bought one called Mabh. She didn't know anything about Mabh as she sprayed the scent over herself and at the candle. Despite the cold it smelled gorgeous. Puff, a face appeared in the mirror and it wasn't hers but a femme fatale, the fairy Mabh. Next doors cat hiding in the bushes yowled and shot up the fence. I know what you want the image said, I will help, and the face vanished.

The old man who lived next door came away from the window disappointed the show was over. Normally he couldn't sleep, hence he often stood at the window or made a cup of tea. But tonight's vision of the girl next door might get him off to an earlier and longer sleep. Downstairs the cat flap banged as his startled cat returned with a secret cat smile.

The very next day Ellie took courage and asked Thomas to take her to the ball, be her date, her beau whatever words she found but could not remember at the time. He agreed, and she gave him that woman's special, look of delight, whimsy, desire and capture, a knowing look which lassoes and brings a man like a calf for slaughter; and did Mabh standing by, laugh at loud and Ellie tremble with excitement.

On that fateful glittering night, Ellie made her lips so red, her hair so blond, her cheeks were blushed and lashes heavy with mascara, her clothes were fragranced with Mabh perfume and her body redolent with expectation. The clothes were carefully chosen from bare skin to coat, in case a chill came in, for Penzance weather is nought but changeable. Heels were high enough to make a mountain goat dizzy. And hold up tights!

The Simmertones had been booked so the music rocked, the band did play, and carousel was the night time play, and Mabh's fairies came and peered and laughed and too played games of love and mischief on this night and new born day.

As much expected, she awoke next morning in his arms. The glamour had worked its strange magic. For glamour past is no look at all hence Mabh's abhorrence of a bright summer morn, for all is blown away. The lips have paled, the blusher ashen or worn away by cheek to jowl. Eyes peer from panda sockets made by shadow and mascara, and a mouth tastes bad from what is best left unsaid.

Thomas stirs and turns, 'OMG you look awful, are you alright' he gallantly asks, a manly phrase calculated to make any girl feel wanted and cared for. She huffed and puffed whilst he is stammering, he fought hard to set matters right by saying the usual reliable man phrase, 'I didn't mean it like that, you always look lovely and all the time. I love you without makeup, just as you are, fresh and wonderful' and that is how the play begins; the dance of boy and girl and ends contrived by fairy lore. It has always been that way as the ancient hieroglyphs and cave art show, all down to this day.

For Mabh of course it was a day to rise from the waters and to contemplate her nights play and wonder what next to do. When first she came this way, the Great Lake was her home and the Lady of the Lake ruled the holy island which happened also to be a fairy court. Not as impressive as fair Tara to the West or Maja's Dun to the South and the Fair Isle of the North but impressive in its setting, the Tor in water and sky nonetheless.

Ever since the men had come to drain the land Mabh tried to spoil their works. They dug their rhynes, ditches and ponds and when they were done, she filled them all with Carey, Yeo, Brue, Isle, Tone, Parrett and the crafty Soy. Once when the fairy land was banished by law and wise women were near drowned to see if they held to the faith of Fay, Mabh brought a great storm. It breached the tidal walls and came as high as church steeples, to remind men that they had more important things to do than mess with poor women. They then had to dig and dig again.

Then came the time of pumps, the sound of which lulls Mabh to sleep in the shallow waters of the night. By day, to amuse herself, she sometimes persuades annoying boys to open sluice gates just for mindless fun. Until of late, men had thought that nature was at rest. The water birds, the fish and furry creatures of the bank and stream had come again, and it seemed man had learned his lesson to let nature be.

The water world is one of balance, give and take. But men are ever greedy, and the good earth nothing more than a source of profit. So, man had pastured his heavy cattle on soft ground, had cut the sponge like peat to the very clay and destroyed with plough the reed and water laden mosses. They built their paths and ways and houses where water needs to flow and so when rain comes to man's hard surfaces, it quickly runs to manmade streams and torrent.

So Mabh delighted when Mother Earth shook herself again and floods came back to the Soy lands draining all to the tidal sea. The land was drenched and became as it should be. Men moaned and wept at flood filled dwellings but lain upon wetland as though it should be dry. Great pumps were brought from far across the Northern sea to spew waters as fast as ever could be, but men still had to wait till Earth was through and water rested again in marsh and bog. As before, men came from far London town to view the waters of the moor take back their runs and ways. They grieved and promised to tear out the rich earth mud and pile it high, dig channels deep, that never again, would let water fairies play or otters roam and water voles nest. It seems true that mortal man never learns from history his puniness, compared to the magic of the land, water, and the air above. So Mabh waits another day.

The lesson of this story is, never play with Mabh for water has its fire; admire her, play her game if you must, but never trust the winter frozen still, iced water, which she may well be under and despite what she may whisper to you, no mortal man or woman can walk on water but can drown.

CHAPTER 8

Graine

Some say at my naming day it was midwinter, so I was called forth for the risen Sun Goddess Graine whose gentle light was just returning, casting long shadows behind the old lichen encrusted standing stones who resonated to her light, and the great holed wheel stone sacred to the far western people. These old stones had lain in place from time before time when giants helped raise them for the little brown people. Graine spoke 'I am no goddess for my people lie in between the worlds of Earth and Heaven for I am of the Fay.'

'I like my name, but others stumble and when they hesitate, I say 'it's said like this Groy/nyeh' so it is not so difficult when one hears how to say the letters. Some say it looks like grain, the barley, wheat and oats that feed the men of the West. They grind the seed to a flour and then bake breads and cake. I prefer the cakes I must say as you shall see. But whatever you call me I am usually close by.'

'I am not a lover of the marshy plains or the high hills but wherever you may find a fairy mound or rath, I and my attendant kin will always be, close by. We, the Fay love the hollow hills and my golden sprite kind are best seen at twilight, at the purple gloaming when the sun sinks and the moon is seen in crescent form.'

The crescent moon is a cup, a symbol of what can be taken, added, fruitfulness, the fullness of the timeless cycle of seasons who defy the exactness of time. Now is the moment not set by moon and stars but set by when the time is ripe alone. When waters seep to the grain and seed and they swell to life in everlasting cycle then is now. That is how Graine is, a giver of herself, to fulfil the dreams of others until the harvest cutting begins when John Barleycorn is spent from her embrace. And then the seed is sown again and all begins anew.

The night is the time for renewal, when the heat of the day has gone and the land sighs with relief. The night waits with bated breath as we fairies shake out our folded wings and flutter cool breaths of air to the night folk and waiting leaves and flowers. The night moths seek nectar and spread the means of life with fluttering silent wings. The perfume of night scented stocks will waft upon the breeze and angel trumpets release their heady fragrance to mix with white lily and the scent of evening primrose, but none can equal the somnolence of sweet jasmine. The scent of the Fay is the redolence of summer eves.

This is the time for all good men and women to end their toil, lay aside the cares of the day and head for home from the fields. But the time we seed and grain fairies like best is when the harvest dust yellows the moon and the barley brew is drunk. Then we steal away some seed to feed the birds of the air who live on the bounty of fruit and seed until the name day of Graine, our mistress and the winter cruelly bites, and the season turns to wait the sun.

'I Graine often hold a lotus at eventide as fragrance is my food, as with the gods of heaven. What art it would be if those baker boys would flavour for me a cake of lotus taste. For taste and fragrance are but one and my tastes are simple, and I am easily pleased. But hark well, this even time is one when mortals fear the fairy mounds and raths, for they know that magic is about.'

The abode of Graine, her home, when not wandering in fields of glowing corn or steppes of waving grass is a simple place, where sky meets sea and the sun sinks into the western sea. It is where humans think Tir na nOg must lie. But the Fay are all around and no amount of wist or wish can place them other than right here just over your left shoulder if you are quick to see.

Fair Boskyny is the place she chose to haunt when at her gold lit rest. Here she lay her silken locks and limbs of honey gold and her lips that dripped of honey taste when kissed in rapture. As night fell, she glowed like electrum as quicksilver moonbeams fell upon her wondrous form. She is a one for rest except when the madness of the harvest must take hold for the harvest yields the mean of life.

Too many piskies play in nearby Dun Tagell or Trevena as is properly called, so she chose this quiet place where travellers pass by north and south. It is naught for her, for she has power to flutter and a trip from her sweet hollow, singing hill to the court of Avalon if called by Oberon and Titania.

She spoke to me these words when I first learned the secrets of the stones. Hear words now as you read.

'Some many years ago, it was nearby, I cast my spells upon the Christian monks who would not believe their eyes, for I would appear from time to time, to tempt them, like a syren by the waterspout with its cloutie ponds and glen. I would gently sing and play my flute and ring a silver bell before they stole it from me, for monks like bells above all ringing things. They called me ghost, white lady and gasped as they saw that where I walked, white flowers would spring up to mark my passing. I used to leave a fairy cairn of my passage close by the waterspout. I built small stone piles in the shallow stream and they convinced themselves of some evil magic.'

The monks soon left this haunted glen for the Western sea shores of stormy Deffon. They fled to the end of the world, to the far rocks before the land sweeps down to Kernow. It is a wild and desolate place where tall tales are told of the ancient monks. One of their brotherhood was a rogue called Nectan. He claimed that his head had been cut off by a giant. Now as the narrator of these events knows that this could not be true for Gogmagog, the last of the giants of Albion was killed by Corineus one of the Trojans who came and founded the land of Britain and all that was long before Nectan's time.

Nectan claimed he carried his head around before sticking it back on! Yet Christians, who believe many such tales, say they cannot believe in fairies, but those were the days of yore I suppose. Somehow, Nectan got to be a saint. Nectan was never there where Graine played and sang, but he spent his life Deffon side. It was his acolytes named her favourite glen of Cornwall for their master whom they greatly feared.

Graine did remember when the Sea People first came to our coves and sandy bays. They lived a while secluded from the tribes when disaster struck their homes. It was they who brought Graine the art of making purple and royal blue robes from the slime of sea snails. She dressed the Fay in splendid colours which the Fay have always loved. Their traders came and went with the swallows rowing in their swift galleys. They spoke of great bulls with sweeping horns and bee queens and the labyrinth where a half bull and human lived. Then one year they came, went as usual but returned unexpectedly before winter.

Their home had been destroyed by a great catastrophe, they were lost, distressed. Graine suggested they stay by fresh water, wintering there and live within this rocky valley where they would be undisturbed by war or grief. And then when spring came, then summer, and no more boats sailed in, they accepted fate and stayed. They carved their symbols on their dancing stage for that was a way for them to worship their goddess; to dance like the mating cranes. As you know Graine is a queen for dancing, as are all fairies, but she is the Lady of the Dance, but I stray from my tale.

For all good mortals know to never disturb a fairy home or sleep on, or by, a fairy mound. Now her place at Boskyny as the years advanced was not so easy to spot amongst the holiday traffic. Indeed, in the 21st century although more people sought the Fay, moving from place to place became a difficult thing to do by carriage. A change of mood had come to the war weary land in the last part of the 20th century. The young had rebelled against the materialism of their governing materialistic men and women and so began to look to other ways to find the peace that excels in mind.

For the Fay like Graine, it was a time of happy irresponsible return. For the young had long locks and wore strange garments from far flung places in multicolours. They played music on guitars, sang songs and sang again, and danced the nights away and found the juice of plants and the magic of fairy mushrooms and sweet toadstools just to see things that were not there, but they knew were really there. They loved in the sun, and again in moonlight. They returned to tending the earth and showed respect for all living things. It was this time, the Oligarch despised and soon this golden age dispersed into the nothingness of mundane working life.

A wandering young minstrel had come by our way of the West and set a trend for living the life of the beach, sand, shore and hedgerow. Many followed in his footsteps, girls and boys; it was a Summer of Love. The old lore's were not well known, although many seekers of the old paths were now reading, listening and learning past secret ways and the craft of the wise.

Now let Graine take up the story for I am tired; 'for some reason, known but to a select few, the 158th day of any year is a special one, as is the preceding evening. For as you may know we count in the land of Fay the old way of time telling. The day does not begin at midnight but at evening fall, so evening to evening. It is especially auspicious if the day preceding falls on the 6th day of the week.

This eventide of a Thursday, a young man unwisely and rudely, without asking came to rest on my fairy mound. It was a pleasant evening after a sunny day, cool but not cold. I drifted upward and looked at him. He was slim with brown hair, not overlong, clean shaven though rough, a striped shirt of dull green and buff, tight wide belted trousers to the knee, then wide flairs although he was not a sailor. His jacket was of a sleeveless goatskin with yellow trimming but smelled of patchouli not goat, for which I was grateful. He was doing what I thought was a poor attempt at some exercises I had heard were popular in a country called India. So young man, I thought, without permission you have chosen my mound to lay your head and now you must join with me in celebration of this auspicious, to some, day.

Overall it would appear this was a boring sort of day for not much had ever happened of great importance on this day except in Jerusalem a long time ago and that was all about Crusades so not relevant to now, except it teaches you lessons. Did I say 158, right, but if you read this in a leap year it will be another day to add. But never underestimate 7 for that is the right day, a complete and spiritual number hence our Court was of that number too. June is a sunny month hence this day will be called one day Chocolate Ice Cream Day, a fact, for I was foreseeing.'

He interrupted Graine's thought process by strumming his guitar. Not so good she thought.

'For if I am to listen to this half the night, I better bless him with some musicality'. She stroked him on the head with her magical sweet lotus, his hat falling to the ground as his head fell forward, whilst she filled his head with notes like minims and crotchets and things, so he didn't ever have to learn them.

Next, she invaded his very thoughts and seemed to appear to him. Seemed to appear, for he had started to smoke a foul-smelling weed. The type that kills brain cells faster than alcohol, hence used a lot by academics and politicians, a mortal had once informed her which is why the Fay only enjoy mushrooms and never weeds.

She told me I crushed the end of the 'reefer' and snuffed it out. He grumbled, took it out of his mouth surprised at seeing a wispy me but when he smoked, he saw strange things anyway, so he was not over bothered. He didn't light up again as he needed two hands for the music.

I wafted more Jasmine at him and I became clearer and clearer in his minds eye. 'Hi, Babe' he said which pleased me as I was really very old and by his obvious interest in my boobs nothing was sagging. I knew that hippy girls were often bare breasted and that this was a novel expression of freedom for girls of that time, so I sort of swayed about to keep him on line.

'Shall we make love, honey child?' I said, 'Come and lie with me and I will write you songs that will make you famous.' I picked him up in my arms and we flew together to the wide sands of Sennen where the dusk was just settling. The gulls were gliding effortlessly home, the rooks, cawing, flew to far away trees and we made fairy love which meant time was frozen. We awoke to see a dozing ginger cat snoozing along the tamarisk hedge line, it was yawning in the last of the sun. In the distance a dragon kite was being reeled in by a father and son, the kite high in the sky, was attacked by the rooks and we lazily smiled together. 'Remember all this,' I whispered, 'Let it come to you in rhyme and verse and song.'

In a dreamy state he asked what day it was. 'Your Thursday still' I said. I gave him a small pebble to turn over in his hands, which as he looked at it, I turned it to a kaleidoscope of colour, reds, golds and yellows like the colours of the dawn. And as we lay together, night brought on its cloak of velvet to the sky. 'This is a moment which will change your musical life,' I told his sleeping form. Check out those words to see the connection.

Who was she talking to, him you or me? Let's not get confused, it could be addressed to you, or then him, ether way the advice is the same. For Graine can be like this, a million separate heads of grass can appear as one wave, yet every blade is individual, separate and so like her thoughts and being.

He had fallen asleep there but of course, when you think about it, he was asleep anyway, so it made no difference.

She continued, 'I looked inside his head and saw as clear as crystal, the pain he carried, not his but that of his forebears who had seen such wars and hardships. He now feared the new mushroom cloud that heralded doom and was brighter than the sun. So, I sung a soothing ballad to comfort him, to match his mood like a transparent man, made of clear crystal who did not want to appear to fly free as a gull, when such freedom was an illusion of political deceit. Better to play with peppermint sweets and candy, and soldiers be just toys, not real. He twitched and jerked in his dreamtime. I soothed his brow, it was time to dance.'

They drifted north in the moonlight to the circle of great magic dancing stones of Stannon, so unfrequented by mankind except for wise women. It was there I danced widdershins in the cold morning with frost fairies all around and where my mind has stayed to whirl. It was the first time I learned the power of dance from another time.

'What a fine dancing circle this is', Graine said, 'a whirling circle it is, for ghosts and spirits, gods and mythic beasts and as it was, our many fairy kind are practicing for mid-summer.' All were dressed in saffron the colours of sun rising and sunset, the colour of ultimate truth where red and yellow combine for ultimate bliss.

'We ate our saffron cakes and laughed, and his melancholy mellowed for such saffron yellow cake can only cheer or mellow moods at whatever age one be. We danced and sung and spun round and round until we all fell down and the roundelay of drum and pipe was still. The Stannon stones ceased their prancing for none are merrier in the land than they. He sighed, and I whisked him away back to Boskiny way and I dropped him hard to teach him never, ever sleep on a fairy mound again.'

The man boy awoke with a start, stiff and with backache as though a horse had kicked him. He looked around for his sailor cap and stuffed it on his tousled hair. He strummed his guitar for his head was filled with lyrics and tunes he had never heard or seen, but what strange dreams he had enjoyed. As he strummed, he saw his finger stained a little yellow. Odd he thought, like real saffron cake. Odd again he thought, for I have never heard of saffron cake. So how do I know what 'tis?

A few months later when telling me of this story Graine said, 'saffron cake like fragrance is a food loved by the Fay of the West and a favourite at Court as he would learn. I am told he or someone like him would become famous as a minstrel and his words enchanting. Well of course I know that, because I enchanted him! So, beware of Fairy mounds for good or ill, enchantment will come your way and time may well be stolen.

CHAPTER 9

Rowena

For of all those who are of the 7 of the Court of the Fay of the West it is I Rowena who are the least seen by mortal eyes. Of the seven I was the first to reach the shores of the land of Albion and so the Court of Avalon. I was here before the giants when men hunted and gathered my wild berries. I saw the great snows melt, the great floods that swept the giant mammoths to their graves. I was here when men dressed in fur and huddled by the fires. I came from lands of ice and snow where reindeer play and eat sweet lichen and fair mosses to sustain them. For many of the northern Fay like nothing better than to romp and play in snow.

My favourite things? One is time to enjoy sweet nature, and to walk with bare feet on frost hard ground, to feel the frosted grass give way to my footfall and the tingle of ice fingers in my toes. And what better than to roll naked, in the cold crisp snow, and make ones skin redden to the brush of birch leaves. It is a time to be alive, to feel in bone and skin, the crispness in the air, to see a breath become like steam or mist, and then it is you may glimpse me in your breath. Yes, just there amongst the evergreen trees, I ran like a deer for refreshing cold times are no times to tally.

My favourite smells are of the winter time for some are green and others cold. Scent is in the air in pine forests and you feel its health, its life, in every fragrance, the sharp tang of pine or the sweet breath of spruce. What better beauty is there than when snow adorns the green branches and sun halos show bright in blue sky. Yet the hint of warmth and the quietness before the leaden skies allow the first flakes to fall has its own quiet beauty.

But a winter wet I avoid, and hide with the birds beneath dense branches of the evergreen shrubs and trees, neath holly or in the ivy or in a laurel hedge or in the dense quiet conifer forests from the ancient times, but these are rare and the haunt of wild cats and such are not kind to fairy folk.

I sometimes shelter with the furry people of the forest in their dens for when the wind blows there is no shelter for the winter beings. My sweet birds are blown from perch and roost and feathers cannot match the chilling death. The wind I hate. It is then, when it blusters and howls, and freezes snow to woolly coats, and slides snow under doors and into roofs, that I snuggle close to fox and squirrel in their homes. Then only am I jealous of my sisters, as they warm themselves within the fairy forge and take the warmth of the stable from horse and unicorn.

To cheer all under heaven, that breathe and fly, or walk and run, I come out with my fairy assistants to paint the berry fruit red, scarlet and deep purple. My berries red against the snow, brings cheer and life, to many kinds who feast on haw and hard drupe and berry. This is when leafless trees stand forlornly, no rich summer or autumn harvest now from them. Their nuts and acorns hidden by those who wisely hide them in stores and cellars. But my berries come, a living store of rations for all to take, through the darkest days, when the sun may weakly peep through snowflakes gently falling, or Jack Frost shakes his fingers to leaves and twigs.

Leafless trees and branches reach for the sky, but nothing comes of their stretching upward, for winter does not hear or see, for she is unfeeling, as she breaks the clods of earth to make them fit for seeds to flourish. In my forest home, my wise green fir and needle green trees, bend low to support and shelter those that lie beneath.

In the Great Yew forest much is afoot, for of all my trees, it is the yew and the holly which I love best and in which I mostly stay. For the holly trees have thorns, and often brightest red berries, if men have planted wisely, both male and female plants or the blackbird and mistle thrush have scattered seed, for in all nature, it takes two to tango, and bring forth offspring of any kind. My berries are for eating, but the seed is hidden small inside, to be scattered in the cycle of nature. The holly spine keeps men women and children from prying too far into the bush to see me, or my friend the cheerful Robin, for the holly has prickles to keep prying eyes and fingers away.

Now as I said I have been longest serving here in this land, and hereabouts, and I have had many names given to me, but presently my name means 'white hair' in the tongue of the Saxon folk who came to this land. It was they who saw me most, for as industrious farming people, unlike the Celtic folk, amongst whom they lived, they used to rise early even in midwinter, to milk the cows and feed the chickens. And as I love nothing more than a frosty morning my black hair was always white with frost rime and through their breath, I was like a white shadow to their sight, seen against the rising sun and hence my native name.

But as I said I love old father Yew. For he has been around a thousand years or more. All trees are sentient beings, like long standing people. The remnants of the Great Yew forest, which covered so much of the island, still can be found on the western edge of South Saxon lands, and I visit there sometimes for old times sake. In Avalon I seek shelter, comfort and peace or rest with he that grows by the Gemini church, dedicated to the sainted Andrew. For this elder tree has much wisdom and visitors sometimes say this is Merlin's tree, but it is not for I know where that really is, and it is a mighty oak.

As you must know, old yew will open hollow, and after so many people have passed over that none remain to measure its time, the yew will form an empty circle as though daughter trees grow around the edge. Be not fooled, for old yew is still one and the centre of this concealed circle, holds the most powerful magic of the earth. As my job is so tiring, I go to the old trees to recharge, tune in to their energy.

I sit in the middle of the circle and just let the power run up my legs, and into my wings, which are usually folded up and out of sight, for I like keeping my feet on the ground rather than flying, which has dangers in the winter when wings have to be de-iced.

The red fruit of the yew is especially beautiful and loved by many birds. It is however a poison to mortal men, and parents soon teach their children to stay away from these lovely, squishy looking fruits. But it is my solemn old tree friend. It has seen almost my life time. The dark green needles are born on the strong long down swept branches. The great war bows of the English and Welsh archers were made of yew, and yet the mellow golden wood makes furniture of the finest. Indeed, the throne of Oberon and Titania are from the yew. When the moon sheds its gleaming silver, then the yew shows dark mysterious and is the guardian of the graves by lynchet gate. And before the Christos it stood bold by every sacred place.

It was by an old yew tree that I first met David who preferred to call himself Deruvid the Druid. It was pollen time and it was the beginning of my holiday, for I keep to myself half the year, hanging and chilling out around the shade of cooling trees, especially evergreens. Now I happen to know quite a lot about Druids, so let's not confuse druids today, with Druids of Old. If druids today, did what druids did back then, they would all be in prison for violence of word and deed. They never recorded what they got up to, so no one really knows but I have seen them come and go.

Let us turn now to my, soon to become acquaintance, Deruvid, who was, quite new to the druid path, having learned his way by book and wrote (keep in mind as I said druids of old never wrote anything down, it was against their religion. All was committed to memory, and memory changes all things, especially as one ages, into a forgery) and now he was after getting some yew pollen dust.

I know not where he had picked this up, but yew pollen dust when thrown on a fire goes up in a puff of coloured flame. Other dusts do the same but yew yields pollen in excess. He wanted to try this round camp fire to impress his friends with what might look like magic or herb craft. He presently earned a living by visiting restaurants and telling tales of Arthur, Robin of the Hood and Cymbeline a once king of the Island of the Mighty when first the Golden people came.

Scattering yew pollen is also a sure way of attracting wood elves. Sneeze three times and if your eyes stream, they appear. Being a tree lover, I get on with them, even those who inhabit the deep dark wood. There are two types of elves though, generally they are an arrogant lot, even more so than we of the hollow hills, and that says a lot. We all know elves have pointy ears, but the nice ones, the friendly ones, have sweet little noses that turn up a bit, or up a lot, especially when they smile. They are usually helpful, and hang around coppices, rather than the deep dark wood I mentioned.

It is worth considering what an ancient deep dark wood really is. They are not so common as a coppice wood gone wild. For wild coppices came when men ceased cutting branches for poles and handles and wooden things. A deep dark wood is one that is very quiet, where there are no ferns or bracken, except along the edge of the few tracks of men and deer, few flowers or grasses grow, but brambly bits to trip you, twisted faces appear to look at you, and twigs will snap loudly as you tread upon them, and only then you feel the watcher, hidden in between the quiet trunks and branches.

Rarely do you see or hear a bird, and the sun does not shine so much. Rarely then, the sun may break through to a hidden dell, often with water trickling to make a mossy bed, but mostly the ground is dry and lifeless These elves of the deep dark wood can look like, and often dress as mortals in garb past or present. They pass you by, as though out walking and hardly acknowledge you, sometimes they don't even smile, and they might have a hound that also does not seem the usual friendly mutt of a mortal walker. Be aware, for you will feel the fairy arrow in your back, but don't look back, for that can be a challenge, walk on and get home quick. If you have a nice carriage, sometimes they leave a mark, like a scratch to warn you not to come their way again.

So, I said to Deruvid at last, talking in his mind, or

David, whichever, 'sit down under the yew and rest a while.' Yew trees are, as I said, not good mixers with humans, and even sitting under them is not the best idea, unless you want a few odd dreams, for they give of an intoxicating, heady, inspiring gas. Of course, he did not hear me out loud, but when a naked woman jumped out, for that is how I like to dress, from the tree in front of him, he fainted. Clearly not the most red-blooded man I have ever come across.

But I brought him around with my sweet body odour which I wafted at him by waving my arms about. My personal smell, but I prefer fragrance, is like a refreshing shower, for it speaks of ferns and moss, yet topped with the hint of pine resin, and the soft fragrance of spruce, a blend that is not sharp yet refreshes and calms.

He came too and looked at me and said, 'I feel ill, I wanna be sick'. 'Not over me you don't, for I am the fairy Rowena, she of the green trees and red berries,'. He fainted again. I splashed some fairy dust over him this time and the bright light brought him around again. 'Are you a real fairy?' he asked querulously. 'Well if you think naked women just drop out of yew trees you must be daft in the head – what else could I be'.

'My own imagination, he said, 'for I am a druid sitting under a sacred yew tree and my imagination can be vivid.'

'Did you feel that?' I asked, swatting him with a holly branch I always keep handy.

'Ouch', he cried looking at the scratches from the prickles on the hand he had held out to protect himself.

'If you were a real fairy you would have a wand, not that holly brush wood.'

She raised the holly again as if to strike again, 'Okay, you have made your point, you are as real as the tree. Hello I am Deruvid the Druid. Nice to meet you, Rowena'.

Still glowering at him, because he did not show any normal reactions to being accosted by a fairy, she went on, 'Well you are a sort of druid, I give you that, but a modernist, and you are not Welsh I can tell that by your

London accent. All the best druids come from Wales and the Cornish are good but not a scratch on the Welsh. I put it down to the water.'

'Well I look the part when in my robes up on the Tor at the solstices.' He retorted.

'Look David err, Deruvid if you like,' she corrected herself seeing his crestfallen face, 'if you want, sit down here awhile and I will tell you the real stories of the druids. I will tell you why they stood on one leg screaming curses at enemies, especially Romans. But as you seem such a sincere millennial snowflake, I will tell you too of their great skill in herb craft and forest lore, of tricks that were no more than science to come, and how to speak the shin signs with fingers when you crouch around a fire. Let me tell you of the potent zephyrs that trees give to the air we breathe. Some are healthful but others drug, pollute or harm like aerosols. Keep away from the grey witch, the walnut tree for she gives off a headache, whilst our yew will fuddle the brain for you to see the golden halos of the sun around a head.'

She spoke then of mistletoe, the winter colour, its leaf shape and berry colour as a symbol of union, and the custom of kissing under it at winter festival time. But its practical use to winter birds was her main concern. And what of nightshade, hemlock and henbane, lords and ladies, wolfsbane and foxglove all a craft for cunning men and druid types. She spoke of that sweet antiquarian cleric, William, whom she had met a few hundred years before. He had played the flute for her and they spoke of Lincoln green and Robin of the Hood.

'Connections dear Deruvid,' she said, 'he made all the connections when he dug into the earth to look for clues and so must you, it is always connections, for that is how our world exists. Sweet William it was, who imagined the druids to life again.'

She became bored and slipped away leaving him dozing under the ancient tree. It was time to gather ingredients for her winter perfume of spice and cinnamon and orange and pine and sweet jessamine and plan to dress the cones of fir trees with white resin and tell squirrels when it was time to feast. Winter needs forward planning, even dressing trees and storing food, and making time for friends and family and feasting. Then it is the Green Knight may come, and mummers play with tambour and flute, and when Rowena sings the roundelays, and the Fay feast and shout and remember all that has passed.

It was in midwinter that men sensed her peaceful presence, her scent, as she stared through windows at the burning Yule log smouldering red amongst crackling pine cones on solstice night, or near enough, and the raising of the evergreen tree the next young morn, or a bit earlier as women dressed the tree with lights and baubles and it did look grand. But all were symbols of renewal and returning light. Womenkind new it was her, the winter fairy time, for every tree held a fairy or her symbol of the evening star on topmost spire of the tree, where she could sparkle the light and send her blessing to each child and home. For Rowena is always the good fairy.

As for Deruvid, he got over his Glastonbury idyll of forced or imaginary worlds, and he became a scholar of herbs and plant flora, taking a degree in bioscience, and writing several pop books to show the value of forgotten medicine and traditional ways. He lost his imagination, and became quite stuffy, and like many authors just regurgitated the same old thing, which of course is the main purpose of a university. Each year though, unbeknown to all, and in secret from those closest to him, he returns to Glastonbury and he sneaks back to an old yew tree whereunder he falls asleep and dreams another book, which he feels he should remember, but cannot quite get it, as it seems forgotten, for that is the secret of the druids, forgottance.

CHAPTER 10

The End

Now the story of the seven of the Western court of Fay is told, but what of Smok?

Each year the Fay meet for seven festivals, and an extra one to make eight in all. The extra one, some men call Candlemas, and is the most forgot by the mortals, unless one counts the other, Michaelmas, the goosey time. Anyways, the seven courts of Britain meet in their domains at each compass point of North, South, East and West as well as Wales, Ireland and far Scotia. The most important of the fire festivals is when the fires are lit on hills to tell the Fay that they might ride out, for it is then, when Holly King and Oak King fight to see who rules the coming half year time.

Smok and fire festivals should go together, this much is self-evident. It used to be a good time to have a dragon about, to light a fire. However, dragons became as we know, a rarity and a dragon without a fiery breath like Smok, some may unkindly think, is no dragon at all.

Smok felt the same, and as a result became quite depressed. True he had found Peter the Painter in Dun Tagell in Another Green World, but even though he modelled for Peter, who was the master of painting dragons, he mostly was on his own.

The Fay always invited him out for their festivals. As they rode out in all their finery, of satin damask costly robes, with jewels on their hands and arms, gold charms in hair, riding beautiful fairy horses with hooves of silver and manes of liquid gold, Smok in multicolour tie dye guise would bring up the rear, strutting and nodding graciously to the fairy tribes. It made him proud and happy for the day. And all the imps in their saffron party clothes would play with him before going back to imp duties.

So one Candlemas or Imbolc if you prefer the old name,

the Courtly Fay, for this festival time compared to others is quite quiet, without so much to do, except sit around and hope the rain stops, unless you are a shepherd looking after sheep, and the Fay being glorious do not do smelly sheep, although they do quite like cuddly lambs. Anyways, they took to talking about cheering Smok, for isn't that the main occupation of fairies to bring happiness?

Oberon had heard on what people call the grapevine, which in Fairy land they call the bindweed line, for it grows everywhere, climbing up and twisting around to see what's what and putting out big bell like flowers of white or cultivated blue and these enabled listeners to hear better what was being said. Oberon had overheard that deep in a forest in the north of Scotia a lonely unicorn, the last of its kind, was living and pining for someone to talk to other than the local fairies. Like dragons, unicorns are not fairies, although they live in the otherworld, the world of the Fay some call Weird. If they were fairies, they would not be called unicorns which is logic in action.

Even fairy horses need looking after, even if they are not messy like ordinary horses, but they liked to be groomed and fed on sweet vernal grass that tastes of vanilla ice cream. So they asked amongst themselves whether a unicorn may eat grass or hay but decided it really didn't need to eat at all. It gets its energy from the sun, probably through the horn they decided.' Much like me', Oberon observed. 'Not true,' said Titania looking at Oberon's empty platter that had been filled with honey, nectar perfumes and saffron cake, 'you eat like a horse'.

They wondered what colour this particular unicorn could be; unicorns can be any colour, from jet-black and brown to dazzling gold, brilliant red or pure white. They usually have blue or purple eyes which are soft and shining of love, for unicorns are pure bred, or bred to be pure, which is their characteristic.

'Legend has it' Oberon said, 'they attract purity and innocence, which is why they get on so well with children'.

'That cuts me out,' laughed Mabh and they all joined in

the amusement, for fairies are certainly not innocent of tricks and charmings.

They talked to Smok about it and he thought it a brilliant idea except he said was not going up there to Scotia again and his big question was, would a unicorn speak garble or speak plainly which question they debated for they understood his dilemma. It was decided as the unicorn being the symbol of what is now Scotland the unicorn would be familiar with Edinburgh, the royal city of that ancient country whose population were generally very nice like unicorns and a bit independent. The way of speech of Edinburgh would be refined to say the least. Everyone knows that Edinburgh is very upmarket. That settled it, a unicorn hunting they would go.

Not exactly hunting but inviting would be a better phrase, for hunting would, legend says, require a virgin which had caused consternation amongst the womenfolk of mankind, so the practice stopped, the hunt, I mean.

An invitation was sent north and soon the Court of Scotia said they would give up the unicorn upon the condition that Smok would not eat it (out of the question for a vegetarian) and that should the unicorn be unhappy amongst southerners it would be sent back in good condition following the fairy returns policy set up years ago by the FU (Fairy Union). This was an international union of Free Fairy Realms to try to have common standards of understandings. It works okay but German fairies are often rather stiff and stomp about a lot liking to be in charge and French ones a bit, well, strutters like a cockerel, rather than stompers. British fairies like the sea water in between the realms as anyone who lives on an island is an islander by inclination.

The point was argued by Oberon that as the majority of Scotian fairies actually lived south of the border there would be no question of concern, for even in the West there were Buachailleen, Brownies, Gnomes, the Rugalach, Heather Pixies, Pixies and they had their own Seelie Courts all giving some allegiance North and to be of the Scotian clans.

And so, after many days the unicorn arrived, and Smok

and the unicorn became friends instantly for they immediately exchanged smiles which were both of the winning type which are sheer magic. The dragon and the unicorn became inseparable. The Unicorn was called Dolina, a good Scots name. First of all, they lived in Glaston but Smok was a bit of a political campaigner, had two opinions on everything and he got irritated as the nature of the town changed which is what towns do over time.

Eventually they moved to the country, settled on a range of hills with a line of sight to the Tor. Their home range was not far from a village close to Glastonbury said to be still part of that sacred temenos or at least on its far edge. So Smok and Dolina resided around if not in Bere Aller, not far from the Long Port on the river Parrett. That town was famous for its Girt Black Dog and they made friends with the hound too for folk got scared of him 'cos he was big, got excited and chased about as he had a bit of spaniel in his pedigree.'

They didn't live in the village itself for if you believe all the folk tales that abound in the Summer county 'them Zummerzet Volk, them be always slaying dragons,' and the village of Aller was no exception. For a certain John Aller it was who poisoned the dragon who lived there. The dragon in its dying breath saw to the end of John too. 'Quits then, serves him right,' said Smok.

Now Smok had fallen out with the Council and sided with the Fay when the council flattened the Mound. What you didn't know about the Glastonbury Fairy Mound?

In the year 1971 the ancient dancing mound of the Fairies of the West was bulldozed flat. It was here that Merlin had lived, some say, in Arthur's time. It was here that Morgause and Arthur slept together by fairy enchantment. Even mortal men who studied such things by digging in the ground saw that this was a mound made by nature, was of great antiquity but had no value to the town except for fairy legend. So, the land of the 12 hides were fairy cursed as all men know. The industrial site that occupies the site today is still visited by fairies and woe beside any occupier who does not respect the Fay.

It is the governance of the town that the Fay cursed roundly not the ordinary townsfolk and the Fay blighted their outlook with short sight. To this day the town has not recovered its earlier time when a prosperous wool town, a market for the rural folk and a town of learning and civil pride. Smok saw its High Street as polluted by fumes and dirt, it's pretty coloured shops in need of constant renewal due to diesel laden dirt. The street furniture vandalised and frequented by unsavoury characters; charlatans and those who practice black arts parade as though in a new age.

The Fay will not lift the curse until the heart of the town is recognised as its people; and they must learn better ways to welcome those who come to the Court of the Fay, ancient Avalon, bringing wealth, and seeking happiness in fine food and drink, song and mirth, philosophy and legend and a time to be at peace and in joy.

'Where can you find such in this wasteland' Smok had argued. But you the reader may seek and ye shall still find the truthful Fay that still try to dance on their mound and fly to the court each festival in the watery glen by Torside both red and white.

Smok still argues too that a gnarly worm is not a dragon. For good townsfolk run the streets each year in a dragon way. 'Not so' shouts Smok as he waddles, 'them bain't no proper dragons,' now portly due to good food. 'Gnarly worms are not dragons,' he shouts, 'Go back to China land, or River Tyneside', he bawls, but no one listens for they are having fun and if truth is known, so does Smok who likes to be contrary.

'We need more people to come to see us Fay', he grumbles to Dolina, all the year round, for all the festivals. He once asked Oberon to lift the curse and then more than once, but he said he will not until the High Street, is returned to the people. 'People must walk freely in the streets and sit at tables and drink good tea and eat cream scones and children wander freely without fear as is the case in most civilised towns and cities of the 21st century' Oberon explained.

'Glaston is not a place for nature lovers, one must look to the moors and the greening Levels where bitterns boom and otters paly. There the true old gods are found, and the Great Queen, the Lady of the Lake still rules but not in the fading town, except for those good folks who hold fast the legend and reality of She. Mostly of womenkind, they strive to keep alive the essence of the power of place and those unseen.

Smok and Dolina maybe found grumbling happily, sitting on the promontory of Turn Hill to enjoy the great view of the Somerset wetlands. Their domain is that of Bere and Aller woods where oak and ash, beloved by magically inclined folk still survive in splendour. Deer roam the woods and badgers frequent the paths and sweet dormice sleep snugly. The Fay are here, and converse with our famous duo. Smok will talk endlessly of the great dragon flag of Wessex and the dragon of Arthur whilst Dolina sings of heather and the weaving of tweed. They are an odd but happy couple.

The best time to find them is when the woods shimmer in a haze of bluebells or when the red mushroom sprinkled white push forth with the ink caps, earth balls and puffballs and the rare earthstar close by elfcaps and stinkhorns so you cannot fail to see this is a place of the Fay, for it is called Turn Hill and so if you turn again, and again, at least thrice times and you may be lucky for the sight may come. If no luck, for luck is a fickle thing, enjoy the view which itself you will see, is quite magical!

Now that is the end of the tale. I, the story teller wishes you joy and sweet dreams, a good night's sleep, good company and health, but nothing comes without the blessing of the otherworld where I belong, so greet you all with the sighing wind as I fade into the sky blue yonder.

AFTERWORD

The 60's and 70's were a time in which the Fay became manifest again. That generation still persists and has seen how politics of green red and blue have continued to destroy the planet in a cloak of greenwash engendering rules, controls authority by fear of the future from natural cycles of which we humans are as dust in time. This generation for all its love of nature has seen plants, animals and the air come to their limits. The Fay or their equivalent or Gaia will end our destruction which may well mean the end of us – never upset a fairy!

THINKING THOUGHTS

Find and play the 'Fairy Tale' or 'Fairy Tales and Colours' for insights by Donovan

Listen to the opera 'The Immortal Hour' by the composer Rutland Boughton first performed in Glastonbury 26th August 1914 the month Britain enters the war.

Be inspired by the artists John Duncan and E.Hornel, Linda Ravenscroft, Anne Anderson, Edward Dulac, David Delamare and more not forgetting Arthur Rackham.

Read W.B.Yeats works and the 'The Golden Bough' by Sir James Frazer.

Read too the words of Jim McGuinn of the Byrds and apply them to yourself and your circumstances or get the track 5D!

For best Dragon pictures visit our great friends www.peterpracownik.com or the Another Green World in Tintagel.

For the summoning Fairy Fragrances and the Ladies of the Lake visioning fragrances go to www.fragrantearth.com or the Fragrant Earth shop in Glastonbury.

About the Author

Jan Kusmirek lives and works in the temenos of the Ancient Avalon, Glastonbury in the Somerset Levels and Marshes. Inspired by the landscape this is his second book about the Otherworld and the Old Faiths and Ways. Well known for his reference books in the fragrance and aromatic world, his expertise in aroma cosmetology is recognised around the world. His lifelong interest in ecology and the human biome and the wondrous interaction of the living planet leads him to say the idea of fairies may be as practical as many scientific theories about sentient beings. His other books are historical novels of the aftermath of WW2.

www.ingramcontent.com/pod-product-compliance
Ingram Content Group UK Ltd.
Pitfield, Milton Keynes, MK11 3LW, UK
UKHW042000230426
12048UKWH00009B/453